RACE to the GOLDEN CITY

BY ALLISON LASSIEUR

SCHOLASTIC INC.

New York   Toronto   London   Auckland   Sydney
Mexico City   New Delhi   Hong Kong   Buenos Aires

ISBN-13: 978-0-439-92328-6
ISBN-10: 0-439-92328-X

12 11 10 9 8 7 6 5 4 3 2 1   7 8 9 10 11/0

Printed in the U.S.A.
First printing, September 2007

CHAPTER 1

It was a desperate situation at the Golden City. Dozens, no hundreds of robots were rushing toward the gates. All the EXO-FORCE pilots stood bravely in the face of the attack. But Hitomi, the newest and most courageous EXO-FORCE pilot, could see that they were all terrified.

"Someone must save us!" Ryo yelled.

"We can't defeat these rust buckets!" screamed Takeshi.

"Who will be our hero?" said Hikaru.

"ME!" Hitomi exclaimed. "I will save the Golden City!"

"Oh, thank you!" Ryo, Takeshi, and Hikaru said together. "We are too weak to fight. You must save us all from the robots!"

Hitomi soared upward in the flying battle machine that had been made just for her. She aimed her turbo blaster guns at the robot battle machines. Bam! Bam! Dozens of robot battle machines fell with every shot. Hitomi laughed aloud.

"Take that!" she cried as she aimed her guns and fired again. "Take that!"

"Take what?" an annoyed voice replied.

"Huh?" Hitomi said, shaking herself. She looked around. She wasn't in the air, saving the world from the robots. She was standing in front of the Golden Tower. Not as a brave EXO-FORCE pilot. No. As a lowly tower guard.

"Stop daydreaming and pay attention," the voice said. It was Takeshi. Hitomi's stomach

flipped with embarrassment. Of all people to catch her daydreaming, Takeshi was the worst. "I could have walked right past you and you'd never know it. What kind of guard are you, anyway?"

Hitomi bristled. "If you had to stand here all night, bored stiff, you'd find something to think about, too," she said.

"Really?" Takeshi said. "Maybe I'd be thinking about, oh, guarding the tower."

Before she could think of a good reply, he brushed past her. "I warned Sensei that putting you in a uniform was a bad idea. Good thing you're not an EXO-FORCE pilot. We don't have room, or time, for daydreamers." With that he strode through the door into the Golden Tower.

Hitomi trembled with fury at Takeshi. "Who do you think you are?" she sputtered. But she knew who he was — one of the star EXO-FORCE pilots in the fleet. He, along with Ryo, Hikaru, and Ha-Ya-To, were the best of the best. More than anything, Hitomi wanted to be one of them.

All she ever thought about was EXO-FORCE. Since she was a little girl she had dreamed of being a pilot. But her grandfather, Sensei Keiken, had other ideas. When she had begged him to let her join the EXO-FORCE team, becoming a guard was not what she had in mind! How could she ever prove to him that she could be a true EXO-FORCE pilot if she was stuck here all the time? Hitomi sighed.

"I'm going to make Sensei understand that he can't hold me back forever!"

Finally, the city bells chimed the hour, signaling the end of her shift. Relieved, Hitomi

raced straight to Sensei Keiken's office in the Golden Tower.

Her grandfather was sitting at a large desk, surrounded by blueprints, diagrams, and half-completed models of different robots and battle machines.

"Granddaughter, come in," Sensei said with a warm smile.

"I came to talk to you about the EXO-FORCE team."

"Ah," Sensei said. "Here we go again." He rose and came to stand beside Hitomi.

"You know I'm old enough to train as a pilot," Hitomi began.

"Yes, you are," Sensei replied.

"I have lots of experience working on battle machines. You know that I was on the design team with Ryo to build and repair them. I still work in the hangars when he needs help."

"You're an excellent mechanic," Sensei agreed pleasantly. "In fact, I'd say you are one of the best battle machine technicians we've got."

"I know I can be a great pilot, Grandfather. I can be one of the best."

"All you say is true," he said. "I'm sure you could be an outstanding EXO-FORCE pilot." Then he paused. "But I cannot stand the thought of losing you in a robot battle."

"No, dear granddaughter," Sensei continued. "No training for you. You are precious to me and I would rather have you safe."

"That's not fair!" Hitomi cried.

"Enough!" Sensei said sternly. "I've made my decision."

How could he! Hitomi thought angrily. She stood, shaking, with her hands clenched in fists. Then a knock came at the door.

"Sensei, I'd like to talk to you." It was Takeshi.

"That will be all, Hitomi," Sensei said. "Come in, Takeshi."

Takeshi stopped short when he saw Hitomi.

"Don't even start," Hitomi grumbled as she strode past him. "I'm not in the mood for your jokes."

Takeshi's eyes widened in surprise as Hitomi left, slamming the door behind her.

Outside, Hitomi slowly slid to the ground, leaning against the door. She was too disappointed and tired to get up. She was out of ideas.

Inside, she could hear Sensei's voice. "I don't understand how that could have happened."

"We don't either," Takeshi said. "Until now, the computers have given us the coordinates with no problem."

"Show me," Sensei said.

Hitomi jumped up. She pressed herself against the wall and held her breath. Sensei and Takeshi burst through the door and disappeared. They hadn't seen her.

Quickly, Hitomi followed them. Sensei and Takeshi were too deep in discussion to notice. Soon they were in the main computer center of the Golden City. Banks of screens lined the walls. In the center stood the large mainframe computer.

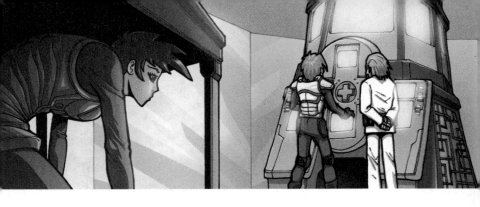

Hitomi ducked under a desk, out of sight, and listened.

Takeshi tapped on the keyboard. Then he said, "See? The computer stops in the middle of the download. It's like something is jamming it."

"Has the programming been checked?"

"Yes, several times," Takeshi replied. He pulled a sheet of paper from the printer. "The coordinates seem to come through fine, though."

"Seem to?" Sensei replied. "What if the malfunction has affected the coordinates? They could be wrong."

"I doubt it," Takeshi said. "The computer has always been right before."

"We shouldn't trust these numbers until we know the computer is working properly," Sensei said. "If these coordinates are wrong, we could be walking into areas crawling with robots."

"I disagree," Takeshi said. "If we don't move now and get the new code, the robots might beat us to it. The EXO-FORCE team is willing to take the risk."

"But I'm not," Sensei said firmly. "No, we'll wait until the computer is repaired. Then you can go."

Hitomi could hear them arguing as they left. She smiled to herself. Takeshi may be arrogant, but he was no match for her grandfather's stubbornness. She crawled out from under the desk and stood up.

On the desk was a piece of paper. It had a series of numbers printed on it. The coordinates!

In a flash, Hitomi knew what she was going to do. She would go after the code herself! What better way to prove to Sensei that she could be a pilot? She would return to the Golden City with the code and be a hero! Even Takeshi wouldn't be able to tease her then. If the coordinates were wrong, no harm done. She'd be back by morning.

"Either way, it's better than guard duty," she whispered to herself as she headed toward the battle machine hangar.

She knew that no one would be at the hangar this late at night. Sure enough, the huge hangar was empty. Hitomi noticed three battle machines in a far corner of the hangar. Two of them were in pieces. One seemed to be in good shape.

"Hm, probably not tested yet," she said to herself as she climbed aboard. "No one will miss this one." Quickly, she powered up the machine. It hummed to life. Hitomi scanned the control panel. Most of the controls looked familiar. She'd been secretly studying all the pilot training manuals for months.

"This must be one of the new battle machines Ryo was working on," she thought. She punched the coordinates into the navigational computer. Accepted! "Well, looks like I'm going *somewhere*."

The streets of the Golden City were quiet. Hitomi piloted the battle machine out of the back gate of the city. The guards didn't stop her. Why should they stop a battle machine? This was too easy.

As soon as she left the gates, she throttled up the machine. It sped away from the Golden City, toward a distant mountain area. For the first time Hitomi became worried.

"Where am I going?" she wondered aloud.

To her complete surprise, the battle machine's comlink sputtered to life. "Nowhere, if I can help it," a familiar voice replied. Hitomi looked out. Standing in front of her was Takeshi in the Blade Titan. And its guns were aimed straight at her.

CHAPTER 2

"Where do you think you're going?" Takeshi's voice crackled over the comlink. "And stealing a battle machine, too?"

"I'm not stealing anything," Hitomi replied angrily. "I'm going to bring it back. And besides," she added, "what are you doing here?"

"None of your business," Takeshi said.

"Hey! You're using the coordinates to find the code yourself! Does Sensei know you're here?"

The comlink was silent.

"He doesn't!" Hitomi shouted. "Ha!"

"You'd better go back, or . . ." Takeshi growled.

"No," Hitomi replied flatly. "Besides, if I go back I'll tell Sensei what you're doing, and he'll throw your sorry self in the brig for a month."

I've got to get out of here before Takeshi reports me, Hitomi thought. She flipped a couple of switches that said "turbo."

"This should get me out of here quick," she said aloud. Instead, the battle machine lurched into the air and floated upward.

"Whoa!" she cried, grabbing the throttle.

"Hey! What are you doing?"

"I don't know!" Hitomi cried. "I'm not sure how to drive this thing!"

Hitomi looked around. The view was great from up here. But she noticed something several miles away.

"Takeshi, I see a strange light over the ridge,"

"Robots," Takeshi said. "It must be. I've got to stop them."

"I'm coming with you."

"I don't have time for this," Takeshi said. "Go home!" And with that he disappeared toward the light. Hitomi slowly pushed the throttle, and to her delight, the battle machine flew forward. She powered off all the lights of the battle machine so the robots wouldn't see her coming. Then she flew quietly toward the light. Below, she could see Takeshi slowly approaching the robots as well.

"Takeshi? You there?"

"Yes. How many?"

"I see five in a small clearing. One battle machine and four drones."

"Piece of cake. Stay put. Try not to do anything stupid."

"Takeshi, no!" Hitomi said. "They haven't seen us. We can sneak past them."

Takeshi ignored Hitomi and inched the Blade Titan closer to the robots. They didn't seem to see him coming. Takeshi burst into the clearing, guns blazing. The drones exploded in a burst of metal and fried circuits. A second later Takeshi's deadly blades sliced through their battle machine armor, sending pieces flying.

"Yeah!" Takeshi yelled over the comlink. "See, I told you, these rust buckets are no match for a real EXO-FORCE pilot!"

"It was too easy," Hitomi said.

"You call that easy? Facing five robots?" Takeshi said.

"Yeah, compared to facing hundreds," Hitomi said. "Look!"

To Hitomi's horror, robots poured over the hill behind them. A dozen robot battle machines rushed toward them, with too many drones to count following behind.

"Time to go!" Takeshi yelled.

Hitomi didn't have to be told twice. She throttled up the machine and sped away from the robot army. Below, the robot battle machines opened fire on the Blade Titan. The Blade Titan was hit several times, but Takeshi kept moving. He returned fire, hitting a couple of the battle machines and sending a squad of drones flying into the trees.

Then he turned and ran. The drones gave chase, but eventually turned and headed back. Hitomi breathed a sigh of relief.

By now streams of smoke and flames were coming from the Blade Titan. Finally Takeshi had to stop. Hitomi landed her battle machine nearby.

"I caught a couple of nasty hits," Takeshi said.

Hitomi ducked inside the smoking Blade Titan. "You've got a fried computer board and some toasted circuits," she called. "Nothing too serious. I'll have it fixed before you can say 'rust bucket.'"

Takeshi paced and grumbled. Soon Hitomi reappeared. "All good," she said, smiling. "All I had to do was . . ."

"All you had to do was go home!" Takeshi yelled. "Look at the trouble you've caused! Now an army of battle machines sits between us and the Golden City, and we have no way of getting back or warning Sensei!"

"ME?" Hitomi yelled back. "YOU left without permission, too. YOU took the coordinates without telling anyone. YOU were stupid enough to call attention to us by attacking a group of robots. YOU got your battle machine shot up. I fixed the Blade Titan and saved your arrogant butt!"

They glared at each other, standing toe to toe.

"I would really like to drop-kick you back to the Golden City," Takeshi finally said.

"Yeah, well I'd like to feed you to the drones," Hitomi replied. "But it looks like we're stuck with each other." She stepped back.

"The Titan is ready to move," she said. "What do you say we go find the code?"

Without a word, Takeshi climbed into his battle machine.

"Try to keep up, then," he said over the comlink.

"You're welcome," Hitomi replied as they set off toward the unexplored lands of Sentai Mountain.

CHAPTER 3

Meca One stood silently in front of the large mainframe computer in the main robot command center. Around him, the center hummed with the activity of hundreds of robots. But Meca One ignored the noise. He was deep in thought.

It was a blow when the humans took over the Golden City. He had not expected them to be strong enough. But Meca One had a plan. It wouldn't be long before he launched a huge attack against the humans and the Golden City — one that he had been planning for months.

Not everything was ready, though. Meca One reached a golden arm over the main computer keyboard and pushed a few buttons. Instantly, a small screen lit up. Meca One peered at the screen. It showed a large mainframe computer and a wall of screens behind it. A few humans were working at keyboards around the room.

But Meca One's attention was fixed on one human who stood beside the mainframe computer. *I see you Sensei Keiken*, Meca One thought. *But you don't know that I see you.* In fact, Meca One had been monitoring Sensei and the humans for a long time.

I wonder how you would feel if you knew that I used one of your own inventions to spy on you? Meca One thought. *Or that your computer was downloading the code coordinates directly to me?*

Meca One pushed another button, and a series of numbers flashed on the screen. These latest coordinates had him worried. Very worried. He recognized these numbers. They led to a code that was so dangerous that no one should ever get it, especially the humans. This code could mean total destruction for the entire robot race. But as long as the humans' computer appeared to be malfunctioning, the humans would not dare trust the numbers and try to find the code. All Meca One had to do was delay the humans for a little while longer.

A message light flashed on the control board. "Field operation to Meca One. Field operation to Meca One."

"What do you have?" Meca One replied.

"Robots are moving into position around the Golden City. A squad of drones is dispatched to retrieve the code. All programming is complete."

"Good," Meca One replied. "Any signs that you have been detected?"

"Negative," came the reply. "Two battle machines attacked a small squadron of drones. One was damaged. Both fled."

"WHAT?" Meca One yelled. "Did they return to the city?"

"Negative. They fled into the wilderness. It is likely they are destroyed. Humans are not programmed to survive in the wilderness."

Meca One slammed his golden fist into the control panel. "NO!" he shouted. "Follow them! Find them! Destroy them!"

Sensei has outsmarted me, Meca One thought with fury. *He has sent the EXO-FORCE team to recover the code after all! They must be stopped. For good.*

Meca One grabbed the intercom microphone. "Attention all robots," he began. His voice echoed throughout the facility. "We are preparing for our biggest attack against the humans. They control the Golden City. Now they are close to finding a weapon so huge that it will destroy the robots for all time. We MUST NOT let them get this weapon. It must be ours!

"Two EXO-FORCE battle machines have been sighted leaving the Golden City. They must be found and destroyed. I am deploying several Mobile Devastators into the field immediately. Their mission will be to eliminate the EXO-

FORCE pilots before they can return the code to the Golden City. Meca One out."

Meca One threw the microphone onto the control panel with a clatter. *They will not get the code,* he thought, *even if I have to destroy them myself.*

CHAPTER 4

Hitomi and Takeshi stood near the top of Sentai Mountain. The area was filled with rocky out-croppings and snow-covered peaks. The wind was cold and the air was thin. Hitomi wondered if humans had ever lived this far up on the mountain.

"This can't be the right place," Takeshi said.

"We programmed the coordinates into our navcoms, and they told us this was the right place. If the numbers are correct."

Neither wanted to say it out loud. Maybe Sensei had been right — the computer malfunction did mess up the coordinates. Hitomi scanned the gray, hard landscape. If a code were here, where would it be?

"Let's look around," Takeshi said. "We've come this far."

"What are we looking for, exactly?"

"Anything that looks out of place."

They steered their battle machines carefully over the rocky landscape. The land felt lost and empty. They searched for several hours. Finally Hitomi said, "My navcom says we're on top of the right spot. See anything?"

Takeshi scanned the area. "No," he sighed. "As much as I hate to admit it, Sensei was right. There's nothing here."

"I don't think it's worth looking anymore," Hitomi said dejectedly. "But I don't want to travel back to the Golden City in the dark, either."

"I agree. There's a small opening between two peaks a few miles that way." Takeshi pointed. "Looks like a good hiding place for the night."

Hitomi took off toward the opening. When she got there, she stopped short. Takeshi was right behind her.

"What the —?" he said, surprised.

Before them was a small valley, completely hidden by the tall peaks of the surrounding mountains. At the bottom of the valley stood a village. A human village. Hitomi whipped out her electro binoculars and scanned the village. Takeshi did the same.

"I don't see anyone," he said finally.

"No robots, either, that I can tell," Hitomi replied. "I see several burned-out buildings, though."

"Me too," Takeshi said. "Must be from the Robot Wars. I'll bet this village was attacked and abandoned then."

They made their way down the valley and into the village. They parked their battle machines and jumped out. The streets were completely deserted. Several buildings were blackened and charred by fire. The mountain wind whistled through the ruins.

Hitomi shivered. "Creepy place. Don't like it."

"Me neither," Takeshi said. "But at least we'll have some shelter from the wind inside one of these buildings."

He tried the door to the nearest building that was still intact. "Locked," he mumbled. Takeshi tried to break it down. It didn't budge. "That's strange," he said as he examined the door. "This door is nailed shut. From the outside."

"Look at this," Hitomi said, motioning him to follow her. Fire had destroyed one wall of a building. She picked her way through the debris until she was inside what was left of the structure.

"See? This building has a door and two windows on the outside. But inside, there's only a blank wall. The windows and doors are fake!"

"All these buildings are fake," Takeshi exclaimed. Sure enough, as they looked closer, they saw that the buildings were little more than flimsy boards hastily nailed together.

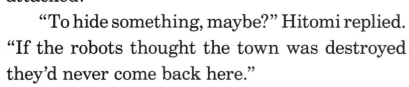

"I don't get this," Takeshi said, puzzled. "Why would someone build a fake town, then burn it to make it look like it had been attacked?"

"To hide something, maybe?" Hitomi replied. "If the robots thought the town was destroyed they'd never come back here."

Then she understood. "Wait. I get it. The coordinates were wrong, but not by much. The code is here."

Takeshi's eyes widened as the realization dawned on him. Then he grinned. "Not bad. For a girl."

"Not bad is right, metalhead," Hitomi replied. "Now start looking for that code!"

They went back to the center of town. They opened every fake building and searched everywhere. Nothing.

Hitomi spied a small storage unit at the end of the main street. It seemed more solid than the rest of the buildings in town. The door seemed solid. It felt real.

She quickly pried the lock off the door. Inside it was dark. There was no floor, only a hole. A ladder descended into the darkness. From somewhere at the bottom of the hole, Hitomi heard a low hum.

"I found something," Hitomi called. Takeshi came running.

"It's probably an old sewer," he said, peering down the dark hole.

"Well, let's find out!" Hitomi grabbed the ladder and stepped down into the darkness.

"You ARE crazy!" Takeshi said.

"Yeah, but the question is, are you crazy enough to follow me?" Hitomi replied with a grin.

CHAPTER 5

Hitomi shivered in the inky blackness. As they climbed deeper, the hum got louder.

"Ow!" Hitomi cried as Takeshi accidentally stepped on her hand "Watch where you're putting that foot!"

"Sorry," Takeshi said. "I can't see a thing in here."

Hitomi looked down. Far below, the blackness turned to gray. "I think I see a light," she said.

"Keep moving then," Takeshi said.

Rung by rung they made their way down. Finally they

reached the end of the ladder. Below her, Hitomi could see a shiny floor. She held her breath and jumped.

The drop wasn't far and she landed feet first. Immediately she drew her energy katanas, which she always carried. Takeshi dropped beside her, his guns ready.

A soft light illuminated the small room where they landed. The floor and walls were made of some kind of metal. There were no doors anywhere. A long passageway stretched away from them. The humming noise was coming from the end of the passage. The only other way out was back up.

"Doesn't look much like a sewer, eh?" Hitomi said sarcastically.

Takeshi glared at her but didn't reply.

Hitomi smiled to herself as they started off. At the end of the passageway they came to a large metal door. Takeshi tried it. It swung open silently, revealing a large room. Two narrow passageways stretched out of the room in opposite directions.

"Now what?" Hitomi said.

"We'll split up," Takeshi said. "It'll be faster that way. Keep your personal comlink on at all times. I don't want to lose contact."

"I don't like this," Hitomi said. "We should stay together."

"Afraid?" Takeshi replied in that familiar tone that Hitomi hated. "Should have known you don't have the courage to be a real EXO-FORCE pilot."

"I'm not afraid!" Hitomi said. "But I'm not stupid, either. Separating is a bonehead thing to do, and you know it. This place could be crawling with robots!"

"Then I suggest you keep your eyes open and your energy katanas ready," Takeshi called as he ran down a hallway. "Be back here in half an hour!"

Hitomi sighed. Takeshi was always taking unnecessary risks. She made her way down the opposite passageway. It looked just like the last one — long and metal, with a door at the end. But the humming was getting louder.

Slowly she approached the door. The sound was so loud that she could feel its pulse in her body. She pushed the door open, then gasped at what she saw.

She was standing on a small landing high above the biggest room she'd ever seen. Several battle machine hangars could easily fit in here, with room to spare. Everything  was bathed in a soft green light. Huge computers — bigger than she could have imagined — filled the space. Lights flickered and flashed on countless screens and control panels. But there was no one here, no humans or robots.

A narrow metal staircase led from the landing down to the floor. Just as she began to take the stairs down, her comlink crackled.

"Checking in," Takeshi said. "All clear here. I'm at the end of the hall, and there's a door."

Before she could reply, Takeshi shouted, "I'm under attack!" Several blasts echoed in the background.

"I'm coming!" Hitomi yelled. She pounded down the metal hallway, katanas ready. Ahead of her, she could hear blasting and the sound of screaming metal.

She turned a corner and ran headlong into three robots. They looked like drones but were smaller and lighter. All three of them turned and opened fire.

One shot clipped Hitomi's comlink, but the rest missed. Hitomi dashed back around the corner and grabbed the half-melted comlink.

"Takeshi, do you read me!" she yelled.

"Yes," his voice crackled. "They're headed toward you. Do you see them?"

The robots rounded the corner.

"Oh, yes. I'll try to hold them off, get over here!" A screeching sound came over the comlink, and then it went dead.

The robots jerked to a stop for an instant. Then they seemed to rev back to life.

"AHHH!" she yelled, slicing the weapons arms off the nearest robot. They fell to the floor with a metallic clatter. The other two aimed at her and fired. She jumped out of the way, and with a quick flick of her wrists she took the heads off both robots at once. The heads skidded across the floor and bounced off the wall, their circuits popping and sparking.

Takeshi appeared. He surveyed the scene with surprise. "You took them all down? I don't believe it." There was a note of respect in his voice that Hitomi had never heard.

"What, didn't think a girl had it in her?" Hitomi replied. "Well, think again, metalhead."

Then she paused. "It was weird, really," she said, kicking the burnt metal circuits of the robots with the toe of her boot. "They stopped just as they saw me, like they were surprised or something. It gave me just enough time to attack."

"Robots can't be surprised," Takeshi said firmly. "You must have been dreaming."

"I don't think so," Hitomi said slowly.

"We don't have time to think," Takeshi said. "I found the code."

They headed down the hall. At the end was an open door. The room was empty except for a metal stand in the center. A small clear box sat on the stand. Inside it, a golden brick shone. There were numbers engraved in the gold.

Takeshi tried opening the box. There didn't seem to be a lid.

"Liquid crystal," Hitomi said, picking up the box. "You can't open it. It'll have to be melted away." She tucked it safely into her uniform.

"Well, that was easy," Takeshi said. "Let's get out of here."

"You won't get any argument from me," Hitomi replied as they made their way to the door. "Not this time, anyway."

CHAPTER 6

By the time they reached the surface it was day-light. As they powered up their battle machines, Hitomi called Takeshi on the battle machine's comlink.

"I've been thinking," she started.

"Don't hurt yourself doing that," Takeshi replied.

She ignored him and continued. "I think our comlinks did something to those robot sentries back there."

"That doesn't seem possible," Takeshi said. "Our comlinks are designed not to interfere with any other systems."

"I know," Hitomi replied. "But still . . ."

"Talk to Sensei about it when we get back," Takeshi said. Then he paused. "If he'll talk to us, that is."

Sensei! She'd almost forgotten that she was going to be in big, big trouble when they got back. She wasn't even sure that finding the code was enough to save her from her grandfather's anger.

As they made their way out of the village and down the mountain, Hitomi was deep in thought. She knew there was something about their comlinks that disabled those robots for just a few seconds.

"But what?" she said to herself. "How?"

Suddenly her battle machine shuddered. Then it shuddered again. Hitomi jerked out of her daydream.

"Drones!"
Takeshi yelled.

The valley in front of them was filled with thousands of drones. There were more robots than she'd ever seen before.

Several dozen huge vehicles were lined up in front of them. On the top of each one was a nasty-looking laser cannon aimed directly at them.

"What the heck are those?" Hitomi cried. Then an explosion rocked the valley. Drones went flying. The Blade Titan was blown back. Hitomi almost lost control of her battle machine.

"We've got to get out of here!" Hitomi started firing wildly into the sea of moving metal. A few drones exploded, but hundreds more kept coming.

"They're going to surround us!" Hitomi cried.

"Keep firing," Takeshi said. "Aim for those Mobile Destroyers. We can't let them fire on us again!"

Hitomi and Takeshi fired everything they had on the vehicles. One by one, they exploded. But the drones kept coming.

"I've got an idea!" Hitomi said, firing again. "I think our comlink frequency stalled those robot sentries. Turn the Blade Titan's comlink to channel twelve, the same one we were using in the village."

"Okay, okay, it's there," Takeshi said, firing all the guns on the Blade Titan at once. Another Mobile Destroyer went up in thousands of broken metal bits.

"Now what?"

"Um, we talk to each other?" Hitomi said desperately.

"Oh, THAT'S going to stop them? We're going to bore them to death with chatter?"

Hitomi looked out at the wall of drones. They kept moving forward.

Takeshi saw them, too. "Great idea," he said. "It's so good, it's going to get us fried."

Hitomi's heart sank. She had been sure that the comlink was the key to disabling the drones. "Let me think!"

"Thinking time, over!" Takeshi said. "Fighting time, NOW!" The Blade Titan rushed into the coming wave of drones, blasting away.

"Another idea!" Hitomi cried. "Keep them distracted!"

"Uh, not a problem!" Takeshi called. The sharp blades of the Blade Titan flashed in the morning sun as he sliced through the drones. More came flooding over a ridge. He wasn't going to last much longer.

Hitomi yanked the throttle and her battle machine lurched into the air. She flew to the nearest canyon wall and aimed her blasters at a huge rocky outcropping. Bam! The shot broke off the huge boulder and it crashed

down. A few hundred drones were crushed like bugs beneath it.

"Take that, metalheads!" Hitomi cried, aiming her blasters at another boulder. Instantly it broke away from the mountainside and flew down onto the drones, missing the Blade Titan by a few feet.

"Hey, watch where you throw those things!" Takeshi yelled.

"Get ready," Hitomi called. "I'm going to build a road out of here!"

Carefully and quickly she aimed her blasters at the cliff face and fired in a straight line down the rock wall. The side of the cliff peeled off in an enormous flat expanse of rock. Slowly, it toppled, rumbling and groaning. It hit the ground with a thunderous roar, making the earth tremble and sending clouds of dirt and dust into the air. Thousands of drones and several Mobile Destroyers disappeared beneath it.

"Your road sir!" Hitomi shouted gleefully, flying over the huge expanse of rock that now cut a huge path across the valley floor.

"Unbelievable," Takeshi said as they fled.

"You're welcome!" Hitomi replied.

"Don't get cocky, though," Takeshi said. "We've still got to get through the robot army and warn Sensei. If the robots haven't already attacked, that is."

"I know," Hitomi said. "We're not out of this yet. Look behind us!"

The drones had regrouped and were coming after them. A dozen or more large Mobile Destroyers were following them. A few shots whizzed past Hitomi's battle machine.

First one to the Golden City wins, she thought grimly.

CHAPTER 7

Hitomi had never moved so fast in her life, but it didn't seem fast enough. Her battle machine was clearly not ready for the kind of abuse she was putting it through. Its engines whined and sputtered, and several times it dropped out of the sky, almost crashing. It was all she could do to control it.

She fought the controls as she flew the battle machine right above Takeshi, firing at the drone army whenever they got too close. He piloted the Blade Titan expertly over the landscape, but the rocks and hilly terrain slowed him down. A battle machine was designed for fighting, not long-distance hiking. Smoke poured from the Blade Titan in several places. Stopping to fight would be suicide. All they could hope for was to make it to the Golden City before the drones overwhelmed them.

"How are you doing down there?" Hitomi called. "Holding together?"

"Barely," Takeshi replied breathlessly.

"Keep moving," Hitomi said, blasting a Mobile Destroyer and sending several dozen drones sailing into the air. "I'll keep them off your tail for as long as I can."

"You better," Takeshi said.

Another voice came over the comlink. "Base to battle machines! Base to battle machines!" Hitomi knew that voice.

"Sensei! It's Hitomi!" she called frantically. "We've got a million drones on our tails. We need help! Repeat, we need assistance!"

"Hitomi!" Sensei yelled. "Where are you?"

Hitomi glanced at her navcom. "Not far from the city gates. We should be there any minute."

"We're under attack," Sensei said. "The robots have surrounded the city."

"Oh, no," Hitomi whispered.

As Hitomi and Takeshi approached the city, the full impact of Sensei's words hit them full force. The beautiful golden city was completely surrounded. Thousands of drones poured out of dozens of Mobile Destroyers. Lines of robot battle machines were attacking every EXO-FORCE battle machine. The EXO-FORCE pilots were no match for the sheer numbers of drones they faced. It was only a matter of time before they would be overwhelmed.

Hitomi looked behind them. The drones were almost on them. A few minutes and they'd be swarmed. The damaged Blade Titan didn't have a chance, and they both knew it.

"Hey," Takeshi's voice came over Hitomi's handheld comlink. She grabbed it off her belt.

"I can't believe this thing still works," she said, staring at the melted plastic.

"My main communications systems are fried. Don't tell anyone I said so, but you'd have made a decent EXO-FORCE pilot."

"No!" Hitomi cried. "I'm not saying good-bye yet!"

The comlink screeched with feedback from its damaged speaker.

"That's IT!" Hitomi said. "It's got to be."

Quickly she hooked up her handheld comlink with the battle machine's control panel. She turned on the outside intercom and cranked up the volume. Then she pressed the button on the handheld.

SCRREEEEEECH! The piercing sound echoed through the air outside. The drones behind them slammed to a stop.

"Fire, Takeshi!" Hitomi yelled. "Fire NOW!"

Takeshi opened fire on the now-still drones. Drones exploded everywhere. Hitomi aimed her guns at the Mobile Destroyers that had also stopped dead. Powerful explosions rocked the area as each one was blasted into pieces.

"Go to the city!" Takeshi said. "I'll finish up here."

Hitomi punched the throttle and the battle machine heaved forward. She still had her hand on the button of the handheld comlink, and the high-pitched screeching sound reverberated through the air. She flew above the robot armies and around the robot battle machines that surrounded the Golden City. As she passed over the drones, the pitch scrambled their circuits and they slammed to a stop. The Mobile Destroyers also stopped. The robot battle machines staggered forward and shot wildly into the sky.

"EXO-FORCE team!" Hitomi yelled. "Destroy the robots!" Immediately the battle machines smashed through the drone army. Laser cannons from the city walls took out the Mobile Destroyers. EXO-FORCE pilots took out the robot battle machines, knocking them to the ground in chunks of smoldering metal and wires. The few that were left turned and ran.

"Heeiay!" Ryo's voice came over the comlink. "We got 'em!"

"That was some crazy trick, Hitomi," Hikaru said. "How'd you do that?"

"Skill and talent, metalhead," Hitomi replied.

Sensei's voice came over the comlink. "Where is Takeshi?" he asked in a calm voice.

"Here, Sensei," he replied. The Blade Titan appeared behind Hitomi. Several blackened holes dotted the machine, and smoke was pouring out of it. But it was still standing.

"How did you know it would work?" Takeshi asked.

Hitomi paused. "Because I'm good," she replied with a smile.

CHAPTER 8

The city was in chaos by the time Hitomi and Takeshi got their battle machines into the hangar. When they finally stepped down from their battle machines, Hitomi and Takeshi were lifted onto the shoulders of the crowd and carried straight to the Golden Tower. By then the rest of the EXO-FORCE team had caught up with them.

"How does it feel to be a hero?" Hikaru said, clapping Hitomi on the back so hard that she staggered forward.

"'Pretty good," Hitomi gasped.

"Don't let it get to your head, kid," Takeshi said. But he was smiling.

Hitomi couldn't wait to see her grandfather. All her wildest dreams had come true! She had completed a dangerous mission and saved the city. He had no choice now but to make her an EXO-FORCE pilot.

When she saw Sensei, she rushed into his arms. He grabbed her in a fierce hug. Then he pushed her away.

"What were you thinking?" he said sternly. "Stealing a battle machine and walking straight into a robot army!"

"And YOU," Sensei turned to Takeshi. "You're one of my best pilots. I gave you a direct order not to go after the code with those coordinates. You disobeyed me, putting yourself and this city in grave danger."

"But," Hitomi started. Sensei silenced her with a wave of his hand.

"I am of a mind to throw you both in the brig for a month," he said. "I don't care if you did get the code. What you did was wrong and you both know it."

"Sensei," Takeshi said. "May I speak?"

Sensei glared at him, then nodded.

"Yes, what we did was wrong," he began. "I am prepared to accept punishment. But you should know about Hitomi's bravery."

Hitomi's jaw dropped and she stared at Takeshi.

He continued. "She didn't hesitate to go after the code, even knowing that it could be a wild-goose chase. She found the hidden entrance. She figured out that the comlink could disable the drones, when I brushed off the idea."

Takeshi took a breath. "She showed herself to be worthy of the EXO-FORCE team, in every way. Please consider that when you decide her punishment."

Hitomi couldn't believe what she was hearing. The other EXO-FORCE pilots couldn't, either. They looked at each other, and then looked at Sensei. He was staring at Hitomi with a mixture of anger and pride.

Finally Sensei spoke. "Considering the circumstances I am willing to delay punishment. As far as becoming an EXO-FORCE pilot, we'll see."

That evening, Hitomi met Sensei and the rest of the EXO-FORCE team in his office in the Golden Tower for a debriefing. Hitomi and Takeshi told Sensei everything: how Hitomi got the coordinates, how they discovered the hidden passageway to the code, and their desperate race back to the Golden City. When Takeshi described how Hitomi used the rock cliffs as a weapon, all the EXO-FORCE pilots were impressed.

"Good move," Ryo said. "I programmed that battle machine with blast  boosters, glad they came in handy."

When Hitomi described the effect of the comlink feedback on the drones, Sensei looked thoughtful. "The damage to the comlink must have created that pitch," he mused. "I never thought of using sound to scramble their circuits. But I'm sure that they'll be reprogrammed to resist it after this."

"Sensei," Hitomi said, "When we were in the passageways I found a huge room, bigger than a dozen battle machine hangars. It was filled with computers and other machines I didn't recognize."

"You discovered the biggest secret to the Golden City," Sensei replied. "That was the main control center to the entire city. It was built underground, miles away, to keep it safe from attack. As long as the energy center is intact the Golden City will have power."

"Why build the fake town over it, though?" Takeshi asked.

"Your hunch was right," Sensei replied. "If the robots thought it was an old, abandoned village they would ignore it."

"Shouldn't it be guarded?" Hitomi asked.

"No," Ryo replied. "If the robots saw battle machines in the area they'd wonder why. Then it would only be a matter of time before they found the power center and destroyed it."

"Ryo is right," Sensei said. "As it is, the robots think the code was hidden in the ruins of the village. They don't have any reason to go poking around there again."

Then Sensei and the other members of the EXO-FORCE team told their story. A few hours after Hitomi and Takeshi left, robot battle machines began to surround the city. At first no one was too worried. The EXO-FORCE team could take the battle machines easily. Then the Mobile Destroyers began appearing. No one knew what they were, until thousands of drones began pouring out of them.

"The robots have never had a way of transporting such large numbers of drones until now," Sensei said. "Drones don't have much fire power, but their sheer numbers can overwhelm even the best battle machines. We didn't have a chance."

"Until Hitomi and Takeshi showed up, that is," Hikaru said.

Hitomi grinned. Takeshi smiled, too.

"It's time to see what this code is going to tell us," Sensei, said. "Let's go to the tower."

When they arrived, they gathered around the computer and Hitomi handed her grandfather the golden brick with the code. Carefully he tapped out the code on the keyboard.

For a moment nothing happened. Hitomi was afraid that the computer was going to malfunction again. Then the printer whirred to life and began to spit out page after page. Sensei examined the pages with a puzzled expression. Then his eyes lit up and he started to laugh.

"What is it?" Hitomi asked, "Is it a new battle machine?"

"Maybe it's a super weapon of some kind," Takeshi said, looking at the pages. "It looks to be some kind of blueprint."

"It's a better computer," Ryo chimed in, looking over Takeshi's shoulder. "Something that will make the Golden City more powerful than ever."

"You're all wrong," Sensei said, still chuckling with glee. "It's the plans for a robot."

"A robot!" Hitomi cried. "What good will those do?"

"More than you can imagine," Sensei replied. "These are the full blueprints and plans for

Meca One, the golden robot."

Slowly, the full impact of Sensei's words sank in. "You mean we know how he's built?" Takeshi asked.

"Every gear and circuit," Sensei replied.

"How about his programming?" Ryo asked.

"Everything," Sensei said. "These plans are the key to defeating the robots forever. This is Meca One's worst nightmare. If robots have nightmares, that is."

"Hey, you made a joke," Hitomi said.

"Enjoy it, it doesn't happen often," Sensei replied with a smile.

Suddenly the computer sputtered. The screen went dark and the printer stopped.

"I'm sick of this," Ryo said. He crawled under the computer and started pulling out circuits and boards.

"Hey, what's this?" he said. He got up and handed something to Sensei. It was a small metal box with dozens of wires snaking out of it.

"I didn't install this," Ryo said. "It's wired to every part of this computer."

Sensei peered at the box. "It's a bug," he said finally. "I recognize the design. The robots must have been spying on us for weeks."

"This explains how the robots seem to know where the codes are hidden before we do," Hitomi said.

"Well, get rid of it!" Takeshi cried. He grabbed the box and pulled. Sparks flew everywhere.

"Don't!" Ryo yelled. "That thing is connected to every circuit in the computer. If we disable it, it'll destroy the mainframe. We'll never be able to get the coordinates, or input the codes again."

"What are we going to do, then?" Takeshi asked.

Sensei thought for a moment. "Nothing," he said. "We can't destroy the computer. But we can use this knowledge against the robots. As long as they don't know that *we* know they're watching."

"I don't like it," Hitomi said. "That puts the EXO-FORCE team in even more danger, if the robots know what we're doing."

"Then I guess you'll have to go after your pilot's training even harder, to be ready for them," Sensei replied with a smile.

"Oh, Grandfather!" Hitomi cried, grabbing him in a big hug. "Do you mean it?"

"That's your punishment for stealing a battle machine," he said. "You've got to learn to pilot it now."

"Great," Takeshi said. "Next thing you know she'll be wanting her own custom-made battle machine."

"That would be YOUR worst nightmare, metalhead," Hitomi replied. "Besides, if you can do something, I can do it — *better!*"